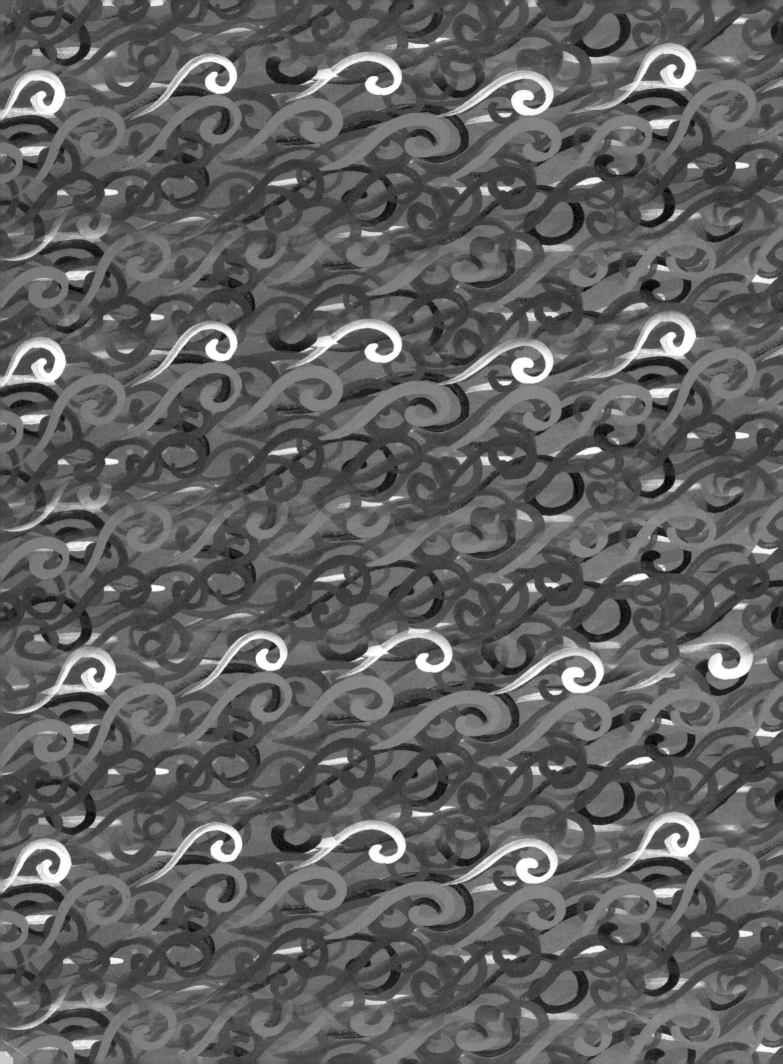

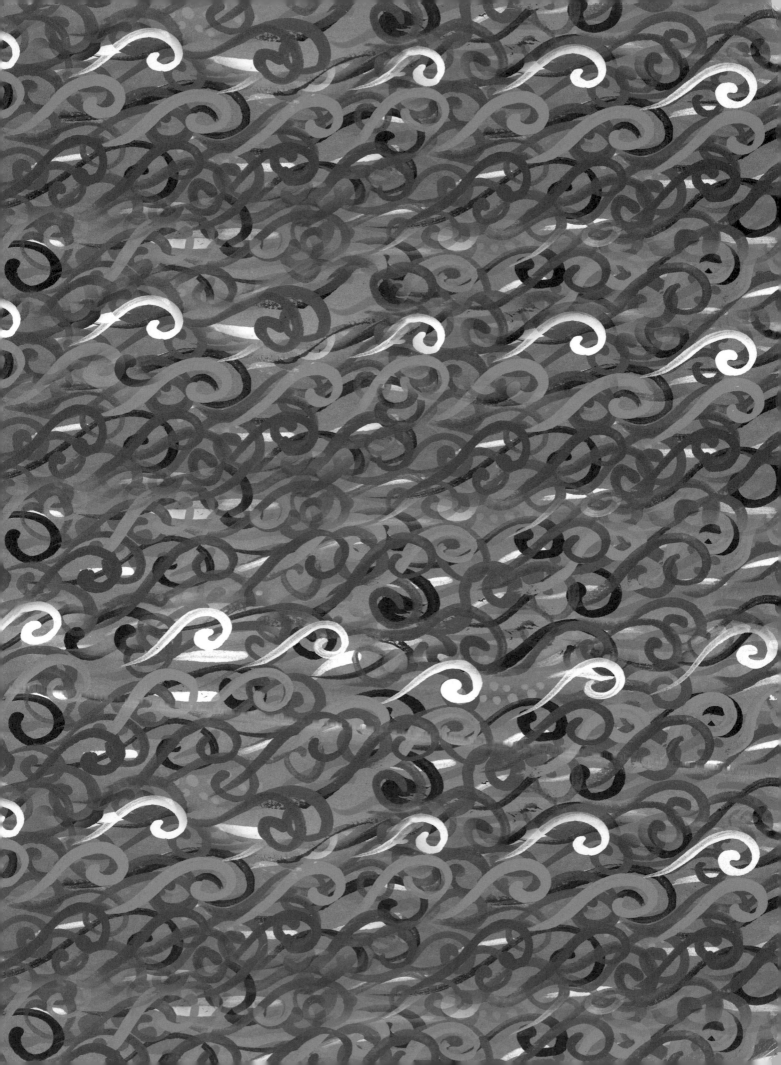

FOR TANNA JAMARRA AND NIA ZSOFIA,
CLARE, KATE AND BEN, BARNABY AND TESSA – KB

Little Hare Books
8/21 Mary Street, Surry Hills
NSW 2010 AUSTRALIA

www.littleharebooks.com

Text by Judith Morecroft
Copyright © text Kaye Bellear 2007
Copyright © illustrations Bronwyn Bancroft 2007

First published 2007
First published in paperback 2008

National Library of Australia
Cataloguing-in-Publication entry

Author: Morecroft, Judith.
Title: Malu kangaroo : how the first children learnt to surf /
author, Judith Morecroft ; Illustrator, Bronwyn Bancroft.
Publisher: Surry Hills, N.S.W. : Little Hare Books, 2008.
ISBN: 978 1 921272 51 6 (pbk.)
Target Audience: For children.
Subjects: Kangaroo--Juvenile fiction--Pictorial works.
Surfing--Juvenile fiction--Pictorial works.
Other Authors/Contributors: Bancroft, Bronwyn.
Dewey Number: A823.3

Designed by Kerry Klinner, Megacity Design
Additional designs by Bernadette Gethings
Printed in China through Phoenix Offset

5 4 3 2 1

MALU KANGAROO

Judith Morecroft & Bronwyn Bancroft

KANGAROO

How the first children
learnt to surf

LITTLE HARE
www.littleharebooks.com

MALU-KANGAROO lived in the wide lands
Beyond the tall tree country,

But he had a great longing for the sea.
So he ran and ran and ran
Until he came to the sea country.

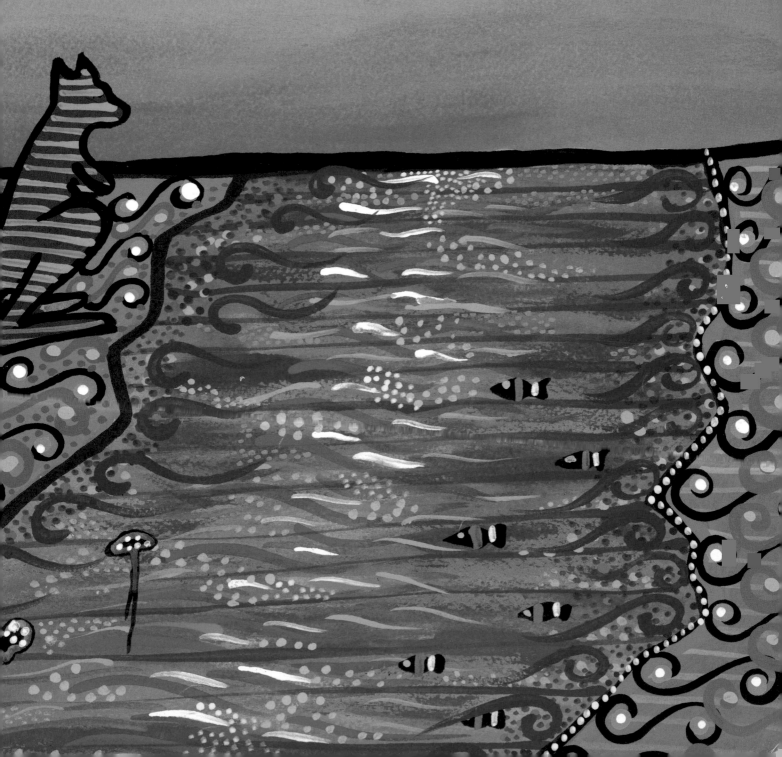

Waiting on the beach were the first children.
"What gift will you give us?" asked the children.

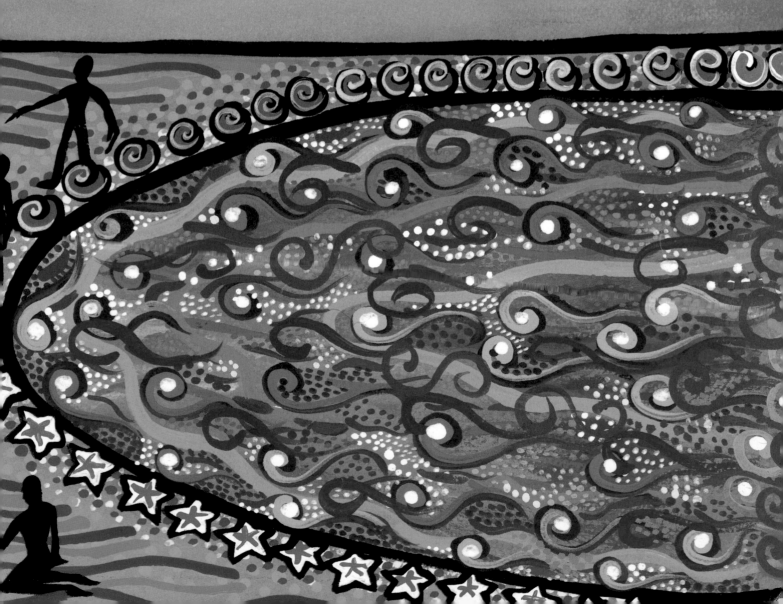

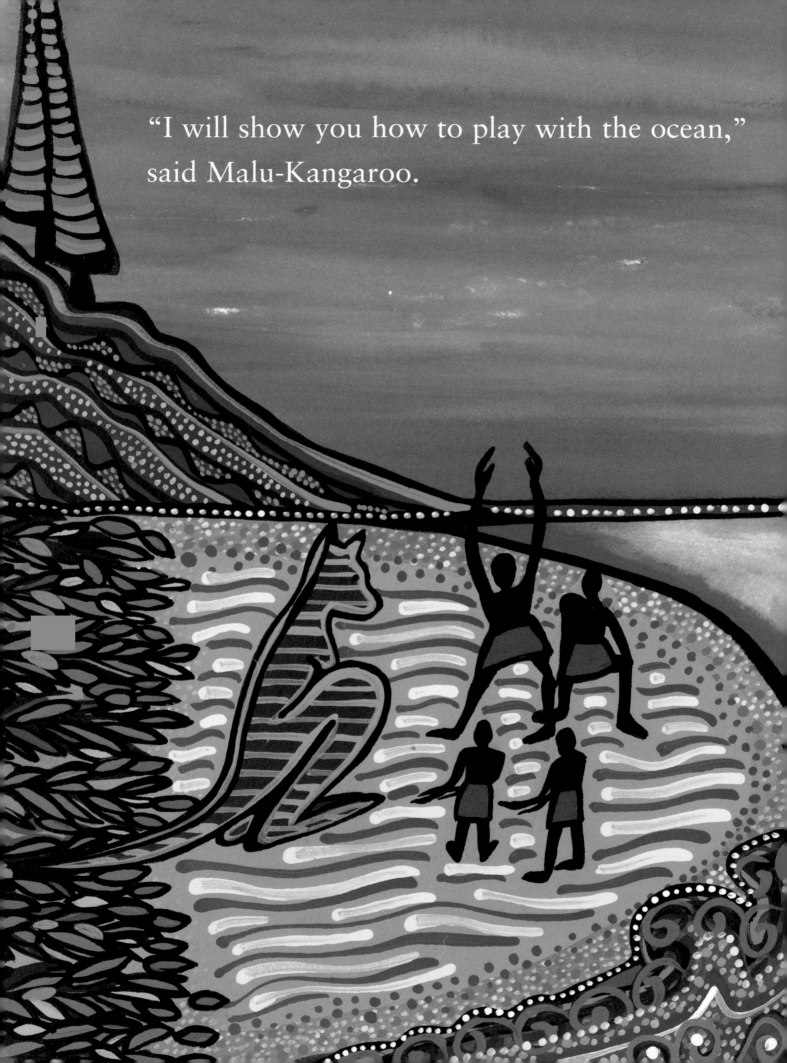

"I will show you how to play with the ocean," said Malu-Kangaroo.

He took some wood and he worked it,
And he shaped it and rubbed it and smoothed it,
And he floated it upon the water
For the first children.

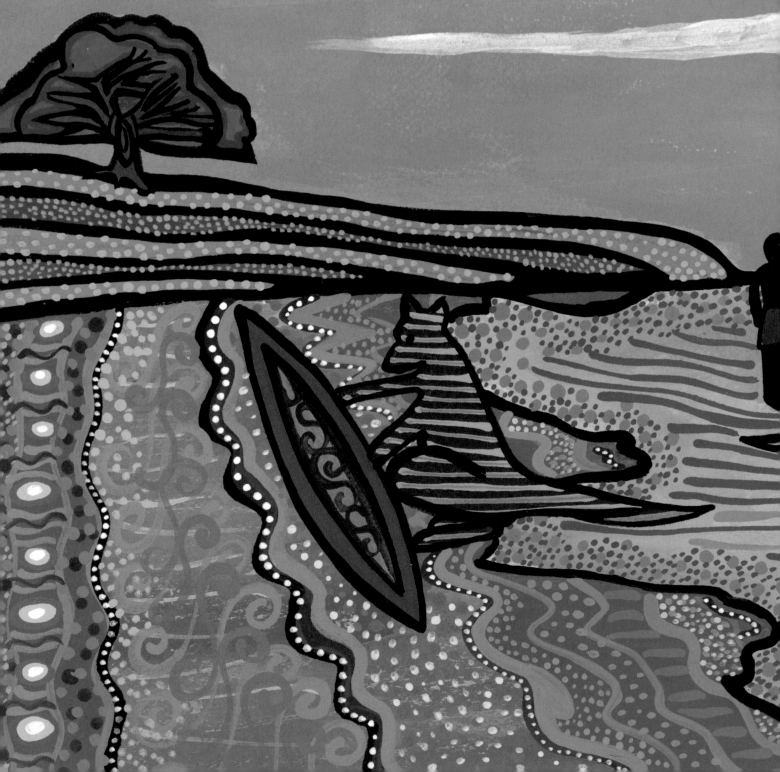

The children took the gift
Of Malu-Kangaroo
And swam out
Into the sea.

They learnt to balance
And to guide it,

They learnt to skim across the water
Like flying fish,

To leap the waves
Like shining dolphins,
And to ride the high crests

Or swoop and fly
Before the crashing breakers
Like bright birds in the sun.

Then Malu-Kangaroo went away to his own place.

But the first children stayed in the sun,

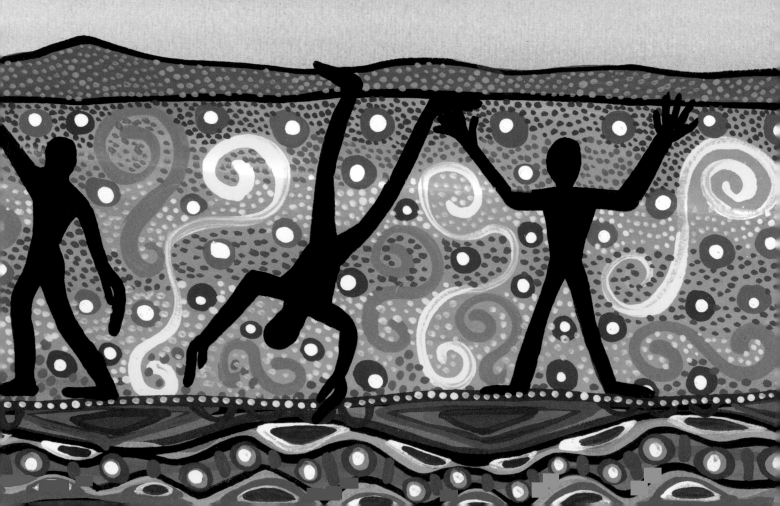

And they played with his gift,
And with the sea.

If you go to the beaches in our time,
Up and down the coast you will see
People surfing.

And you will find
That they skim across the water
And ride the high crests
And fly from the crashing breakers

On surfboards,
Very much like the one
That was first made

For the first children
By MALU-KANGAROO.

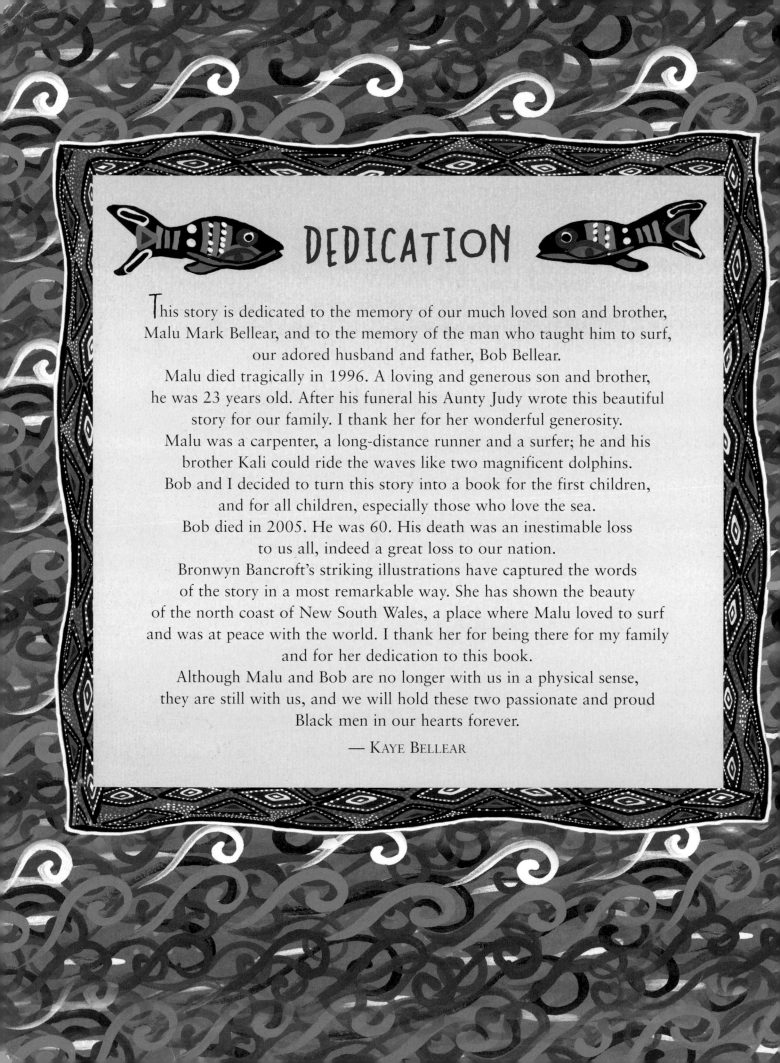

DEDICATION

This story is dedicated to the memory of our much loved son and brother, Malu Mark Bellear, and to the memory of the man who taught him to surf, our adored husband and father, Bob Bellear.

Malu died tragically in 1996. A loving and generous son and brother, he was 23 years old. After his funeral his Aunty Judy wrote this beautiful story for our family. I thank her for her wonderful generosity.

Malu was a carpenter, a long-distance runner and a surfer; he and his brother Kali could ride the waves like two magnificent dolphins.

Bob and I decided to turn this story into a book for the first children, and for all children, especially those who love the sea.

Bob died in 2005. He was 60. His death was an inestimable loss to us all, indeed a great loss to our nation.

Bronwyn Bancroft's striking illustrations have captured the words of the story in a most remarkable way. She has shown the beauty of the north coast of New South Wales, a place where Malu loved to surf and was at peace with the world. I thank her for being there for my family and for her dedication to this book.

Although Malu and Bob are no longer with us in a physical sense, they are still with us, and we will hold these two passionate and proud Black men in our hearts forever.

— KAYE BELLEAR

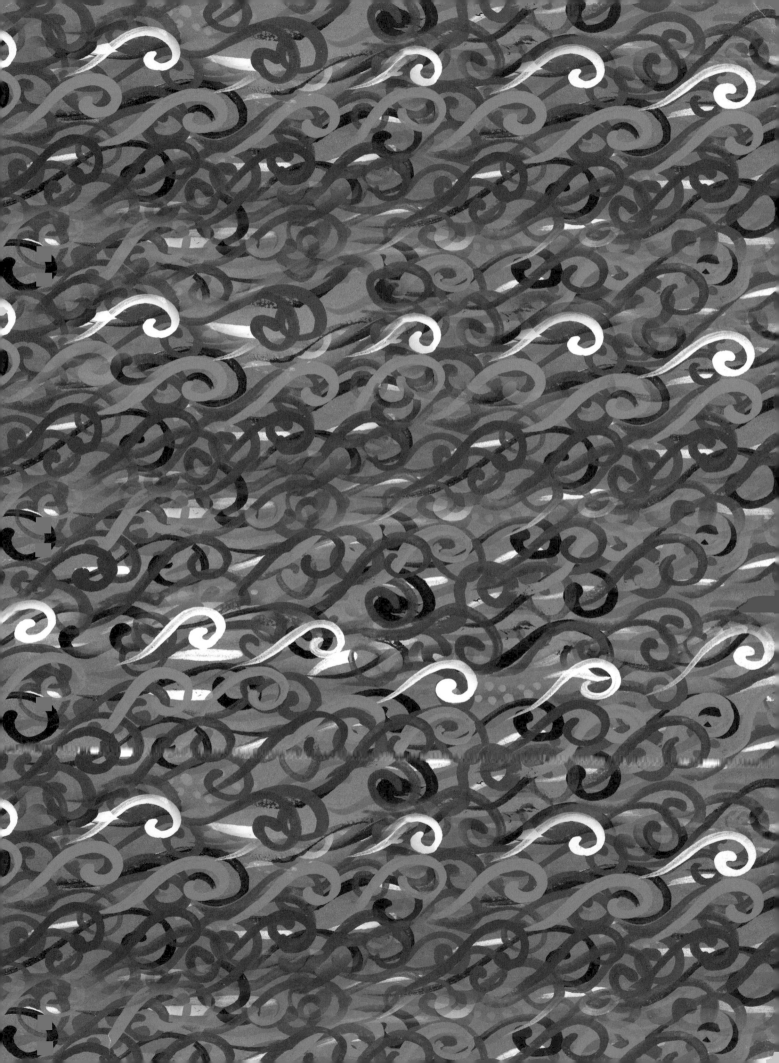

Montem Primary School
Hornsey Road
London N7 7QT
Tel: 020 7272 6556
Fax: 020 7272 1838